Karen S. Robbins | Illustrated by Rachael Brunson

I Think I Can

4880 Lower Valley Road · Atglen, PA 19310

Type set in Archer/Variable

ISBN: 978-0-7643-5691-9
Printed in China

Published by Schiffer Publishing, Ltd.
4880 Lower Valley Road | Atglen, PA 19310
Phone: (610) 593-1777; Fax: (610) 593-2002
E-mail: Info@schifferbooks.com
Web: www.schifferbooks.com

For our complete selection of fine books on this and related subjects, please visit our website at www.schifferbooks.com. You may also write for a free catalog.

Schiffer Publishing's titles are available at special discounts for bulk purchases for sales promotions or premiums. Special editions, including personalized covers, corporate imprints, and excerpts, can be created in large quantities for special needs. For more information, contact the publisher.

We are always looking for people to write books on new and related subjects. If you have an idea for a book, please contact us at proposals@schifferbooks.com.

Do you want to learn to read?

Aardvark and Mouse will show you how!

Grab your mom, dad, grandparent, or friend.

Let your reading buddy be Aardvark,

and you can be Mouse.

Aardvark's words are blue and

Mouse's words are **black.**

Have fun reading with all your friends!

"I think I can."

"You think you can?"

"Yes. I think I can."

"You think you can what?"

"I think I can sing."

"You think you can sing?"

"Yes. I think I can sing."

"What do you think
you can sing?"

"I think I can sing a song."

"You think you can sing a song?"

"Yes. I can sing a song."

"OK. What song can
you sing?"

"It's a surprise!"

"A SURPRISE?"

"Yes, a surprise!"

"Do I have to hide my eyes?"

"No. You must look at me."

"Do I have to plug my ears?"

"No, silly!
You must listen to me."

"Do I have to stand up?"

"No. I stand up.
You must sit in this chair."

"OK.
I'm sitting in the chair.
I'm looking at you.
Let me hear you sing
your song. Let me see the
surprise."

"Sing, sing, sing a song,
Sing along with me.
Sing together, you and me.
Oh, happy we will be.
Read, read, read along.
Read along with me.
Read together, you and me.
Oh, happily we'll read."

"I liked your song."

"Thank you."

"You were right.
You can sing.
You can sing a song."

"Thank you.
You can clap now."

CLAP **CLAP** CLAP CLAP

CLAP CLAP **CLAP** CLAP

CLAP CLAP CLAP CLAP

CLAP CLAP **CLAP** CLAP

CLAP **CLAP** CLAP CLAP

CLAP CLAP CLAP **CLAP**

CLAP CLAP CLAP CLAP

Karen Robbins has devoted her life to children as an elementary teacher, *Romper Room* TV teacher, author, publisher, book/toy designer, and inventor with a US patent. Karen is a right-brain creative whose passion is creating books and toys for children. There are more than 300,000 copies of her books in the world. *Think Circles, Think Triangles, Think Squares, Think Farm Animals, Think Zoo Animals,* and *Flags Across America* are her most recent books. Karen holds a bachelor's degree from the University of Washington and a master's degree from the University of Puget Sound. She lives in Gig Harbor, Washington, and loves presenting to school children to entertain and inspire young minds.

Rachael Brunson holds a BFA from Northwest College of Art and Design and lives in Gig Harbor, Washington, with her two cats, snail, fish, frog, and ever-growing collection of succulents.